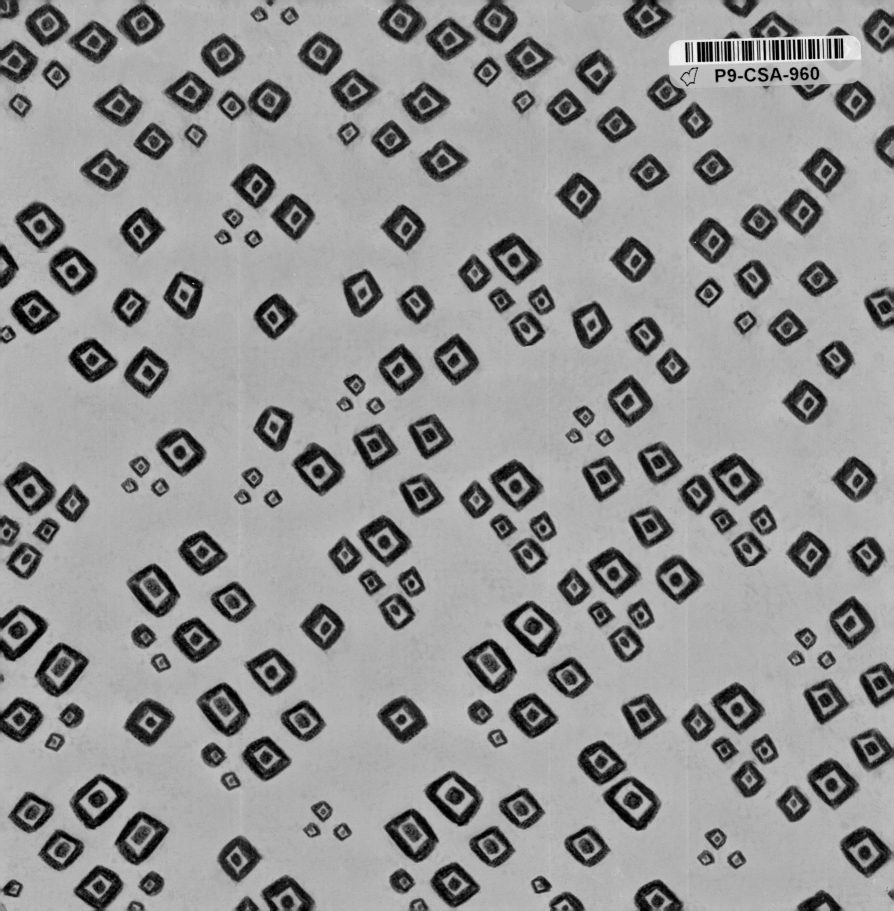

"To my family of storytellers at Story Connection, Singapore,
and my own family: thanks for your love and support."
- Srividhya Venkat

The Clever Tailor

First US print January 2019

Text: Srividhya Venkat
Illustrations: Nayantara Surendranath

Karadi Tales Company Pvt. Ltd.
3A Dev Regency, 11 First Main Road,
Gandhi Nagar, Adyar, Chennai 600020
Tel: +91 44 4205 4243
email: contact@karaditales.com
www.karaditales.com

ISBN: 978-81-9338-890-7

Distributed in the United States by Consortium Book Sales & Distribution
www.cbsd.com

Cataloging - in - Publication information:

Printed and bound in India by Manipal Technologies Limited, Manipal

Venkat, Srividhya
The Clever Tailor / Srividhya Venkat; illustrated by Nayantara Surendranath
p.32; color illustrations; 24.5 x 24 cm.

JUV000000 JUVENILE FICTION / General
JUV048000 JUVENILE FICTION / Clothing & Dress
JUV074000 JUVENILE FICTION / Diversity & Multicultural
JUV013000 JUVENILE FICTION / Family / General
JUV063000 JUVENILE FICTION / Recycling & Green Living

The Clever Tailor

Srividhya Venkat
Nayantara Surendranath

Rupa Ram was a talented tailor.
Everyone loved the clothes he made.

PRAISE..

"That's a perfect-fitting sherwani!"
"Of course; Rupa Ram made it!"
"Isn't this lehenga-choli gorgeous?"
"Rupa Ram has magic in his fingers."

Though he was showered with compliments and requests, Rupa Ram was unhappy.

All his life, he had stitched clothes for thousands of people, but not once for his own family. Hard as he tried, he never had enough savings to buy the best cloth available and stitch something special for them.

One day, Rupa Ram had a wedding to attend. A saafa was a must-wear for men at weddings. All he had was an old, faded saafa. Left without a choice, he went to the wedding wearing it.

At the wedding, Rupa Ram was welcomed with a gift — a brand new

saafa!

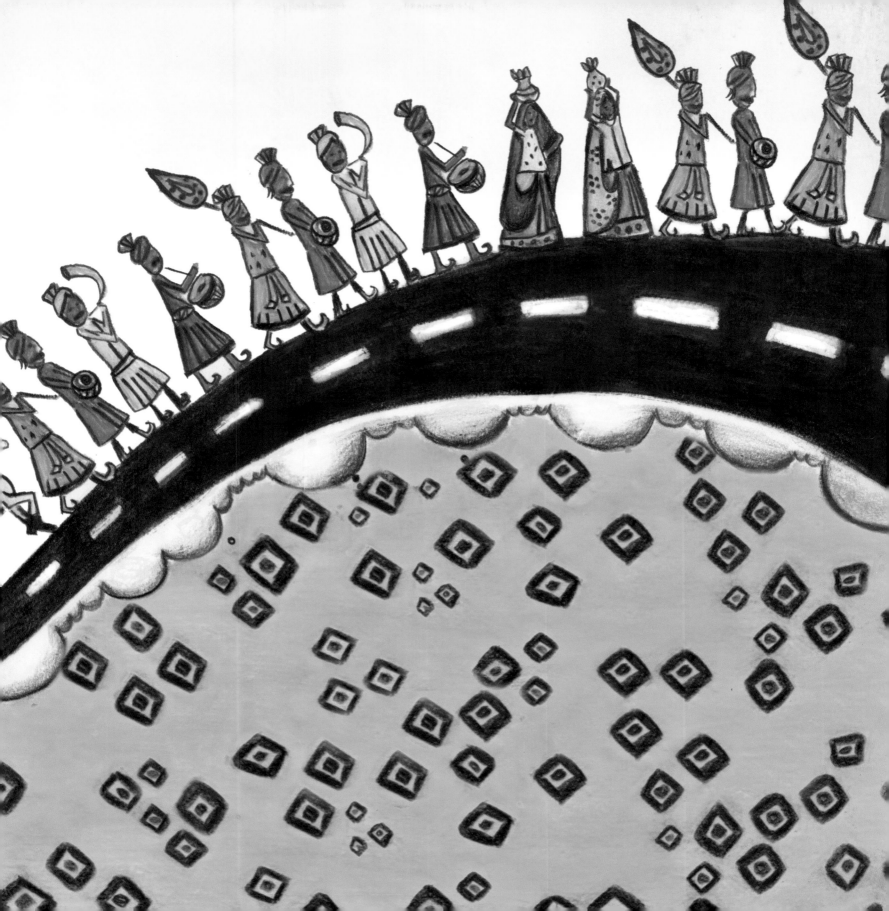

Rupa Ram grew so fond of his new saafa that he wore it wherever he went...
In fact, he used the saafa so much that it finally wore out.

But when Rupa Ram examined the saafa carefully, he found that there was plenty of fine cloth left to make it into something useful... for his wife.

He began to work on it right away. When it was ready, he surprised his wife with... an

odhni!

Rupa Ram's wife was so delighted to have a
new odhni that she wore it wherever she went...

In fact, she used the odhni so much that it
finally wore out.

TAILOR

School...

Helping
Rupa.

But when Rupa Ram examined the odhni carefully, he found that there was still some fine cloth left to make it into something useful... for his son.

He began to work on it right away.
When it was ready, he surprised
his son with... a

kurta!

Rupa Ram's son was so happy to have a new kurta that he wore it wherever he went...

In fact, he used the kurta so much that it finally wore out.

But when Rupa Ram examined the kurta carefully, he found that there was still enough fine cloth left to make it into something useful... for his daughter. He began to work on it right away.

When it was ready, he surprised
his daughter with... a

gudiya!

Rupa Ram's daughter was so excited to have a gudiya that
she took it wherever she went...

In fact, she played with the gudiya so much that it finally wore out.

When Rupa Ram found the gudiya and examined it carefully, he saw that there was still a bit of fine cloth left to make it into something useful... for his family.

He began to work on it right away. When it was ready, he surprised his family with... a

gulaab!

Rupa Ram's family was so proud of the special gulaab made from their favorite cloth that they displayed it in different rooms in the house...

MANDIR

In fact, they used the gulaab so
much that it finally wore out.

When Rupa Ram examined the gulaab carefully, he found that there was still a tiny bit of fine cloth left to make it into something useful... for everyone.

But unlike before, he neither had to cut it nor stitch it because it was ready. He surprised everyone with... a kahaani, a story of how he had transformed his saafa

into an
odhni,

then a
kurta,

then a
gudiya,

and finally, a
gulaab!

Rupa Ram proudly told his kahaani wherever he went and to everyone he met. The best thing was that unlike the other things he had created, his kahaani NEVER wore out.

BEFORE YOU THROW SOMETHING AWAY...

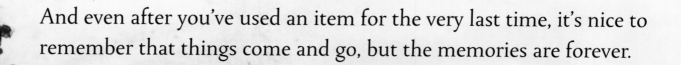

People in India love repurposing various fabrics, often attaching sentimental value to these items that are passed on from parent to child, or from an older sibling to a younger one. Old embroidered sheets turn into quirky new skirts; pillow cases get made into reusable tote bags; well-worn shirts return with renewed splendor when they're sewn into fluffy patchwork quilts just before the monsoon arrives. It is believed that one must throw away a precious household object only when it is truly at the end of its long journey. Until then, it takes various forms and serves different purposes to different people.

The philosophy behind the practice of upcycling isn't just about being thrifty. This custom is also a way of life that places value on things and to the belief that any item should be used to the fullest extent possible instead of being discarded at the first sign of wear and tear.

With every new creation that arises from the fraying seams of its predecessor, there comes a story of ingenuity told with warmth at family gatherings. Many Indian grandparents can tell you stories of how their beloved vintage saris or dhotis became baby clothes for their grandchildren. After all, it's more fun to recycle something you own, by adding your own special touches to it, than to go shopping for something new!

And even after you've used an item for the very last time, it's nice to remember that things come and go, but the memories are forever.

GLOSSARY

Sherwani – A formal suit worn by Indian men, usually for weddings or festive occasions

Lehenga-choli – A festive three-piece dress worn by Indian women consisting of a long skirt (lehenga), a fitted blouse (choli) and a long piece of cloth that drapes over the outfit (dupatta)

Saafa – A turban worn by Indian men at weddings

Chai – Tea

Odhni – A long scarf worn over the head by women

Kurta – A shirt that reaches the knees, often worn with cotton pants.

Gudiya – A doll

Gulaab – A rose

Mandir – A Hindu temple

Kahaani – A story

SRIVIDHYA VENKAT hopped, skipped and jumped careers before she found her most cherished one – writing for children. She also engages in storytelling to spread the love of books and stories.

NAYANTARA SURENDRANATH is a visual artist, illustrator, and animator. She graduated from Srishti School of Art, Design and Technology with a diploma in Animation and Visual Effects. She primarily works with dry pastels, charcoals, inks, and watercolor pencils. She also teaches art as a medium of self-exploration.

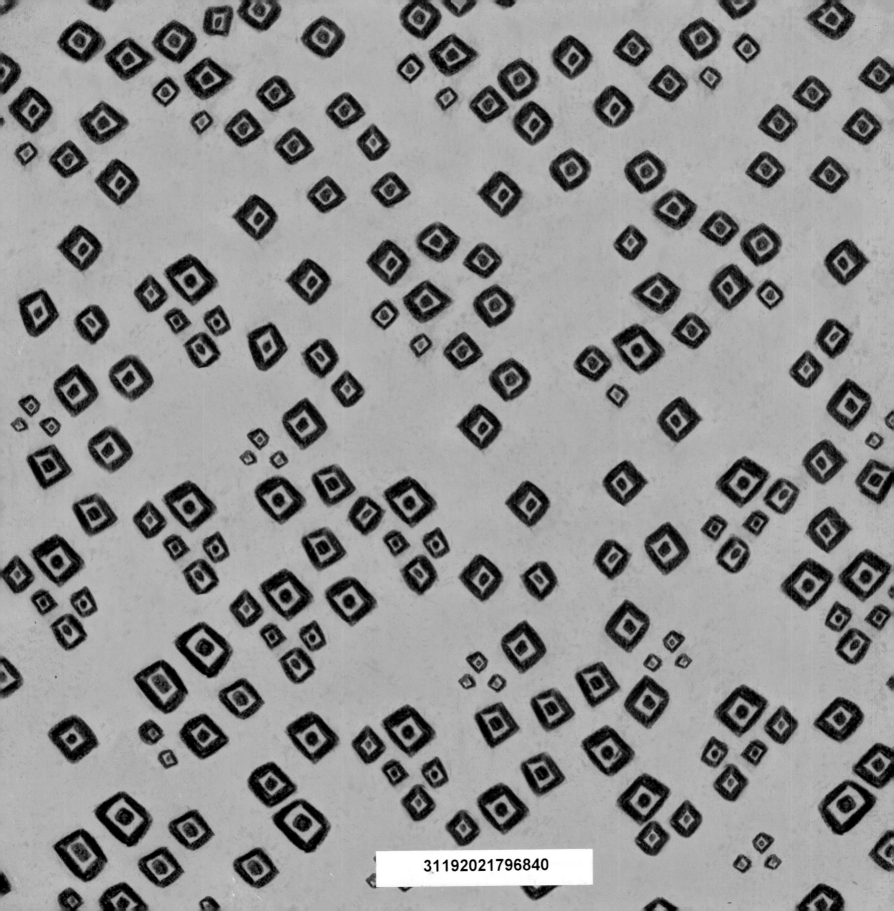

31192021796840